PUFFIN BOOKS

Staying With Grandpa

Born in 1933, Penelope Lively spent her childhood in Egypt. She did not go to school until she was twelve, when her family moved to England and Penelope was sent to a boarding school in Sussex. She then went to Oxford. In 1957 she married Jack Lively, who is Emeritus Professor of Politics at Warwick University. They have a daughter, and a son, and four grandchildren.

Penelope Lively's first children's novel, *Astercote*, was published in 1970. Since then she has written eighteen books for children, two of which have won awards. In 1974 she won the Carnegie Medal for *The Ghost of Thomas Kempe* and in 1977 she won the Whitbread Award for *A Stitch in Time*.

Of her nine adult books, *The Road To Lichfield* and *According to Mark* were shortlisted for the Booker Prize in 1977 and 1984 respectively and *Moon Tiger* won the prize in 1987.

Penelope Lively now lives in North Oxfordshire and in London.

PENELOPE LIVELY

Staying With Grandpa

Illustrated by Paul Howard

PUFFIN BOOKS

For Rachel, Isobel, Jacob
and Anna Penelope Rose

PUFFIN BOOKS

Published by the Penguin Group
Penguin Books Ltd, 27 Wrights Lane, London W8 5TZ, England
Penguin Books USA Inc., 375 Hudson Street, New York, New York 10014, USA
Penguin Books Australia Ltd, Ringwood, Victoria, Australia
Penguin Books Canada Ltd, 10 Alcorn Avenue, Toronto, Ontario, Canada M4V 3B2
Penguin Books (NZ) Ltd, 182—190 Wairau Road, Auckland 10, New Zealand

Penguin Books Ltd, Registered Offices: Harmondsworth, Middlesex, England

First published by Viking 1995
Published in Puffin Books 1997
10 9 8 7 6 5 4 3 2 1

Filmset in Times New Roman

Made and printed in England by Clays Ltd, St Ives plc

Chapter One

Jane was going to stay with her granny and grandpa, all by herself. Her mother said, "You mustn't mind if nothing much happens. Granny and Grandpa lead a quiet life."

Jane had been to stay with Granny and Grandpa often, but other times her father and  mother had come too. She felt very grown up to be going all by herself.

"I'll put plenty of books and games in your case," said her mother, "so you'll have something to do."

The first evening at Granny and Grandpa's house wasn't quiet at all. Jane and Grandpa

played Snap. It was a very
noisy game and they both
laughed a lot. Grandpa
laughed so much he spilt his
cup of tea. Granny said they'd

better stop before everybody got over-excited.

So Jane had a bath and then she went to bed. In the middle of the night she woke up and knew she wasn't at home. Granny came in and reminded her where she was and tucked her up again, and then she felt fine.

Chapter Two

In the morning Jane said, "Is anything going to happen today?"

"Well now," said Grandpa. "I suppose there's always the chance of an earthquake."

"Take no notice of him,"
said Granny. "Maybe we'll go
to the park later. If it doesn't
rain."

So Jane settled down to do
some painting. After a bit she
looked out of the window and
saw Grandpa in the garden.
He was staring up at the roof.
She went out to see what was
going on.

16

"Look at that!" said Grandpa.

There were masses of insects flying about at the top of the house.

"Bees," said Jane.

"No," said Grandpa.
"Wasps. There must be a
wasps' nest in the roof."

"What's the difference
between bees and wasps?"
Jane asked.

"Bees are goodies and wasps
are baddies," said Grandpa.
"Don't ask me why."

"Why?" said Jane.

Grandpa grinned. "Ah. Now
it's funny you should ask. I'd
say, bees sting bad but wasps

sting worse. Or, bees make honey and wasps make trouble. Anyway, it's wasps we've got."

"So what will we do about it?" asked Jane.

"We're going to get the wasp
man," said Grandpa. "This'll
be interesting – you wait and
see."

Grandpa went into the house
and did some telephoning.

After a while the wasp man
came in a truck, with ladders
and tools and drums of spray,
and his son, who was about
twelve and was also his helper.

"If he's the wasp man then

his son is the wasp boy," said
Jane. "What are they going to
do?"

"They're going to find the
wasps' nest and spray it to kill
all the wasps," said Grandpa.

"Poor old wasps," said Jane.

"It's them or us," said Grandpa.

The wasp man set up his ladder and climbed up on to the roof. So did the wasp boy.

Granny said she hoped they wouldn't fall off. She and Grandpa and Jane watched from the garden.

"They won't fall," said Grandpa. "They've been up on

more roofs than you've had hot
dinners."

"Maybe they'll get stung,"
said Jane.

"No way," said Grandpa.
"The wasps know who's boss."

The wasp man took some
tiles off the roof and sprayed
inside. The wasp boy ran up

and down the ladder, helping
him. He ran up two steps at a
time. He ran down holding on
with one hand and jumped the
last bit.

"He's a show-off, that lad,"
said Granny.

The wasp man brought down the wasps' nest. It was like an enormous honeycomb with lots of holes where the wasp grubs had been. The wasp man said that if they had hatched there would have been twenty thousand more wasps.

"Twenty thousand stings!"
said Jane.

Granny made cups of tea for
everyone while the wasp man
put his ladders away.

The wasp boy said to Jane,
"Want to see
what I can
do?"

He stood on his hands and
walked from one end of
Grandpa's garden to the other.
Then he did cartwheels. Then
he did three back-flips, one
after the other. Jane thought
the wasp boy was great.

His father finished his cup of

tea and came out of the house.
He said, "That's enough of
that, you. Time we were on our
way."

That afternoon Jane went to
the park with Granny. She

said, "Did Grandpa discover
the wasps' nest specially
because I'm here?"

"I wouldn't put it past him,"
said Granny.

"I liked that wasp boy," said
Jane.

That evening Jane's mother telephoned. "So . . . what's been happening?" she asked.

"Nothing much," said Jane. "At least . . . there hasn't been an earthquake."

"*What* did you say?" said her mother.

Chapter Three

Next morning Jane said,
"What are we going to do
today?"

"Today," said Grandpa,
"your granny is going to see
Aunt Mary. So we're on our
own, you and me. And I've got
a plan. Ssh!"

When Granny had gone Grandpa took Jane out into the garden. "You know something?" he said. "I'm tired of this garden. This garden has been the same for twenty years."

Jane looked at the garden. It was mostly grass.

"Today we're going to have a go at the garden," said Grandpa. "Before your granny comes back. As a surprise."

Jane said she thought there ought to be more flowers. "You can get plastic flowers. We could plant lots of plastic flowers and then they'd never die and you wouldn't have to water them."

"It's an idea," said
Grandpa. "I could go for it,
myself. But she'd have a fit.
She'd never stand for plastic
flowers."

"We could make a pond,"
said Jane. "And get some
goldfish to put in it."

Grandpa pulled a face. "Too fancy. And I don't want a swimming-pool, either."

"What about a nice big tree," said Jane. "Right in the middle."

"Brilliant!" said Grandpa.

"Why didn't I think of that myself!"

"A big tree would be very expensive," said Jane.

"It would," said Grandpa. "But I think I know where we can get one for nothing."

They got into the car and
Grandpa drove to a place
where some houses were being
built. Everything was being
cleared away to make a space
for the houses.

Grandpa said, "We're going
to rescue a tree that no one
wants, and give it a good
home."

Grandpa had a chat with the builders' men. They were just about to dig up a line of small trees with a bulldozer. They said that Grandpa was welcome to take one of the trees. Jane and Grandpa chose the tree they liked best. When it had been dug up the builders' men helped Grandpa to tie it on to the roof-rack of his car.

Then he and Jane drove back
with the tree waving about on
top of the car. Its roots waved
about at one end and its leaves
at the other. People in the
street turned round to stare.

When they got to the house, Grandpa untied the tree. It was quite heavy, but between them they managed to carry it into the garden.

"Poor tree," said Jane. "It must wonder what's going on."

"Trees don't wonder," said Grandpa. "They just stand there, dropping leaves on people."

He marked out a circle in the middle of the lawn. "And now," he said, "we have to dig an enormous hole for it."

They dug and they dug.

They both got hot and dirty.
Grandpa pretended to fall into
the hole and they laughed a
lot. They found things in the
earth as they dug. They found
broken bits of blue and white
china, and a button that
Granny had lost off her winter

coat years ago. They found a
huge bone.

"Brontosaurus, for sure,"
said Grandpa. "We'll have to
start a museum."

At last the hole was wide
enough and deep enough.

They put the tree upright in the
hole and Jane held it straight
while Grandpa put the earth
back round its roots.

"Whew!" said
Grandpa. "Now
we deserve
some lunch."

"What about the tree?"
asked Jane.

"The tree has water, not
lunch," said Grandpa. And he
told Jane to fill a bucket and
pour the water round the tree's
roots.

"And I'm
going to make
us a fry-up,"
said Grandpa.

"Naughty food. Fried eggs and fried sausages and fried bread and fried tomatoes. Not a word to your granny, mind."

At tea-time Granny came back. She sniffed. "And what have you two had for lunch?" she said.

"Let me see, now . . ." said Grandpa.

"Can't quite remember," said Jane.

"Hmm . . ." said Granny. "And what have you been doing with yourselves?"

They told her to look out of the window.

"Gracious!" said Granny. "However did that get there?"

"It grew, didn't it?" said Grandpa, looking at Jane.

"That's right," said Jane.

Granny went out to have a look at the tree. She said it was a young birch tree and she thought it made all the difference to the garden. She said she simply couldn't imagine how it had sprung up like that from nowhere. She looked very hard at Grandpa as she spoke.

Jane's mother telephoned again that evening. "So what have you been up to today?" she asked.

Jane said she'd been doing some gardening with Grandpa. Her mother said, "Well, that

was nice of you, because I
know you always say you don't
like gardening."

"And we dug up a
brontosaurus," said Jane.

"*What* did you say?" said
her mother.

Chapter Four

Next morning, Grandpa said,
"Today is shopping day. Want
to come?"

Jane didn't usually like
shopping any more than she
liked gardening. But she

guessed that shopping with Grandpa wouldn't be quite like ordinary shopping. "Yes, please," she said.

They went to the supermarket. "The thing about shopping," said Grandpa, "is that it's boring. So you have to

find ways to make it not boring. What I do is – I turn it into a race."

This sounded interesting.

"It's a race against myself," Grandpa went on. "I have to beat my own record. Fill the trolley and get to the check-out

quicker than ever before. My personal best is eleven minutes."

"With two of us we could do better still," said Jane.

"Exactly," said Grandpa.

"Now here's the shopping list your granny's given us."

"You could tell me what to look for," said Jane. "And then I'll dash and get it."

"Just what I had in mind!" said Grandpa.

When they were in the
supermarket Grandpa said,
"I'll push the trolley." He
looked at his watch. "Ten
o'clock exactly. On your
marks. Get set. Go! Fruit and
vegetables first. Apples . . .
bananas . . . potatoes . . .
carrots."

Jane rushed to and fro,
hurling things into the trolley.
"Well done!" cried Grandpa.
"Keep it up! Two minutes
gone!" He whizzed off into the
next aisle with the trolley.

"Next stop cereals and biscuits. We want cornflakes and cream crackers – quick!"

Jane flew along the aisle, with Grandpa galloping after her. "Off to dairy products now!" cried Grandpa. "Butter, strawberry yoghurt, pint of milk . . ."

They hurtled round the corner into the next aisle. Grandpa nearly had a crash with another trolley. "Whoops! Sorry, madam! Five minutes gone now . . . get your skates on, Jane. Washing-powder, Kleenex, polish . . ."

They were both out of breath
now. "What else?" asked Jane.

Grandpa looked at the
shopping list. "Two dustmen
and one roof, it says."

"It can't do," said Jane.
"You don't buy those in
supermarkets."

Grandpa looked at the list
again. "You're dead right.
Can't read your granny's
writing, that's the trouble. Two
dusters and one soap, that's
what it is." He raced off again.

They had finished. They got to the check-out. "Nine and a half minutes!" cried Grandpa. "Terrific! We're the champions!"

"I beg your pardon?" said the check-out lady.

When they got home, Granny
said how nice and quick they'd
been.

"I'm afraid we couldn't get
the dustmen or the roof," said
Jane.

68

"Whatever is the child talking about?" said Granny.

"I can't imagine," said Grandpa.

"So . . ." said Jane's mother on the phone later. "Had a nice day?"

"Grandpa and I had a race
in the supermarket," said Jane.
"*What* did you say?" said
her mother.

Chapter Five

At breakfast next morning Grandpa said, "Whose birthday is it?"

"Not mine," said Jane.

"And it's not mine and it isn't your granny's either," said Grandpa. "But that's too bad, because I feel like making a cake today. It will have to be an *un*birthday cake."

"Am I going to make this
cake too?" asked Jane.

"Of course," said Grandpa.
"I couldn't possibly manage on
my own."

Granny said that she would
go out for a long walk until it

was all over. She said she knew
about Grandpa and cakes.

Grandpa went to the
kitchen. "The thing about
making a cake," he said, "is
that you should never stick to
the rules. Anything goes, that's

what I say." He opened the kitchen cupboard and began to take things out. "Flour. Butter. Chocolate powder. Marmite."

"Not Marmite," said Jane. "Not in a cake."

"I don't see why not," said Grandpa. "But have it your own way. Raisins. Curry powder."

"Not curry powder either," said Jane.

"You've no spirit of adventure," said Grandpa. "That's your trouble. All right then – no curry powder. Now we need a large bowl and two wooden spoons, and we're in business."

They poured and they stirred
and they swished. The kitchen
got in a terrible mess. So did
Jane and Grandpa. When the
cake mix was ready they
spooned it into the biggest cake
tin.

Grandpa put the cake tin
into the oven. "This is going to
be the cake to beat all cakes,"
he said.

They played Snap while the cake was cooking and nearly forgot about it.

"What's that smell?" asked Jane.

"Whoops!" said Grandpa.

They rushed to the oven and

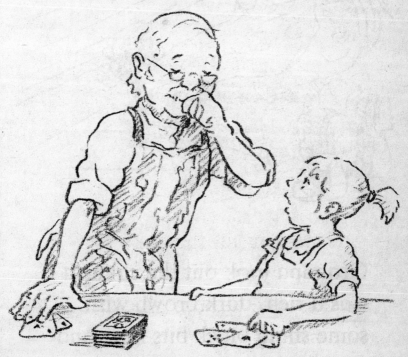

Grandpa took out the cake. It
was a rich, dark brown with
some shiny black bits here and

there. It was much higher on one side than the other.

"Just a touch over-cooked," said Grandpa. "Not to worry."

"It isn't very straight," said Jane.

Grandpa said that made it more interesting. "Any fool can make a cake that's the same all over. Ours is special.

It's got style. Now . . . get
ready to mix the icing."

While the cake cooled they
mixed up icing sugar with
water for the icing. Grandpa
hunted in the cupboard and
found some stuff to turn the

icing pink. He put in a few
drops.

"More," said Jane. "Let's
have a red cake."

Grandpa put in some more
and the icing went a very dark
pink indeed. They spread the
icing on the cake. This took a

long time because the icing
kept slipping off.

At last the cake was covered
all over with very dark pink
icing. There was a good deal of
icing on the floor too, and a
fair amount on Jane and
Grandpa.

"Now we have to write something on it," said Jane. "But it isn't a birthday cake, so what can we write?"

They decided to write SPECIAL CAKE BY JANE AND GRANDPA. Jane did the writing in white icing. She said, "How do you spell special?"

"Not the way you'd think,"
said Grandpa. "It's one of
those dodgy words." And he
told her.

"Now we'd better have a
good clean-up," said Grandpa.
"Or we'll catch it when your
granny gets back."

They washed the kitchen
floor and they washed each
other. And then Granny
arrived back from her walk.

She looked at the cake. "My
goodness!"

Grandpa said, "This cake
slopes from back to front
because Jane and I think that is
an interesting way for a cake
to look."

"Ah," said Granny, "I see."

Grandpa said, "And in case

you're wondering, this cake
does not have curry powder in
it."

"Well, I'm glad to hear
that," said Granny. "I
remember the last one."

They ate some of the cake
for tea and Granny said that
Jane had better take the rest
home with her tomorrow.

"Home?" said Jane. "Am I going home already?"

"You've been here four days," said Granny. "We're going to miss you."

"It doesn't feel nearly as long as four days," said Jane.

"Ah," said Grandpa. "Time can fly, can't it? We have a special kind of day here. Short, interesting days."

Chapter Six

The next morning Jane
packed up her case and put
back the books she'd brought
that she hadn't read and the
games she hadn't played with.
Then her mother arrived

to fetch her. Jane hugged
Granny and Grandpa and
asked if she could come again
soon.

"Any time you like," said
Grandpa. "Next time I'll
arrange for an earthquake."

On the way home Jane's
mother said, "Well, you seem

to have had a busy time. I'm
glad you weren't bored. So
what happened, then?"

"I met the wasp boy," said
Jane.

"You met *who*?" said her
mother.

"And we made a red cake
without any curry powder in
it."

"You made a *what*?" said
her mother.

"And the supermarket didn't
have any dustmen or a roof,
but we found a brontosaurus
bone in the garden."

"Well!" said her mother. "I
don't know how we're going to
keep you amused at home after
all that."

In the evening Granny and Grandpa telephoned to see if Jane and her mother had got back safely.

"Nice to be home, is it?" asked Grandpa.

"It's great," said Jane. "The only thing is, nothing much happens."

Anna, Grandpa, and the Big Storm

Carla Stevens

"Do you think I've never seen snow before?" asked Grandpa. "Anna's going to school, and I'm going to take her. And that's that!"

Anna is determined to get to school for the final of the spelling competition. But as she and her Grandpa struggle through the blizzard, Anna wonders if they will ever get there and, when their train gets stuck, if they will ever get home again!

Also in Young Puffin

ONLY A SHOW

Anne Fine

Anna had told herself a hundred times that it didn't matter – it was only a show . . .

But nothing makes any difference to how miserable Anna feels. Miss Henry had said that everyone in the class had to do a five-minute show and she just can't think of anything. Her mum and her brother, Simon, keep telling her she *is* special, *very* special – but will she be able to prove it to the rest of her class?

A warm, perceptive story from an award-winning author.

The Great Piratical Rumbustification
and The Librarian and The Robbers

Margaret Mahy

Two wildly improbable and wonderfully witty stories.

When Mr and Mrs Terrapin phone the agency for a baby-sitter, the last person they expect to see is a one-legged, one-eyed retired 'naval gentleman'. Unknowingly, they have set the scene for the greatest pirate party of all time! And there's a tale of a lovely librarian who defeats her kidnappers with the aid of the deadly disease called Raging Measles.

Also in Young Puffin

The Ghost *at* Codlin Castle
and Other Stories

Dick King-Smith

Have you ever wondered what it's like to carry your head under your arm? Or tried to guess what garden gnomes get up to after dark?

In this marvellously varied collection of stories, Dick King-Smith introduces some fascinating characters: a baby yeti, a bald hobgoblin and an extraordinary sausage-shaped alien among them.

Funny, mysterious, sinister, these gripping tales make ideal bedtime reading. With remarkable illustrations by Amanda Harvey, this is a book to stir the imagination.

Also in Young Puffin

Fanny Witch and the Thunder Lizard

Jeremy Strong

"Oh dear, oh dear. Don't you see? That monster has eaten my Book of Spells. Eaten it!"

Everybody loves Fanny Witch, the schoolteacher, until she magics up a fully grown, live brontosaurus for the children, and the thunder lizard steals her Spell Book so she can't *un*magic the brontosaurus away.

When the boosnatch comes to the village and steals all the children, Fanny Witch has to come to the rescue!

Also in Young Puffin

SPORTS DAY
for Charlie
Joy Allen

Sports Day is in two weeks' time

Charlie decides Dad must go on a strict training programme in order to stand any chance of winning the Father's Race. And with Charlie entered for four races, excitement mounts until the big day arrives, and the races are for real.

In the second story, Charlie's class visits a Farm Park. With a football-mad donkey and a pickpocket duck, Charlie finds the trip a brilliant day out.

Together for the first time in one volume, these two stories about Charlie's adventures are fun and easy to read.